I Will Try

Marilyn Janovitz

Holiday House / New York

With thanks
to Julie Amper,
my editor

I LIKE TO READ™ is a trademark of Holiday House.

Copyright © 2012 by Marilyn Janovitz
All rights reserved
HOLIDAY HOUSE is registered in the U.S. Patent and Trademark Office.
Printed and Bound in November 2011 at Tien Wah Press, Johor Bahru, Johor, Malaysia.
The typeface is Report School.
The illustrations were created with pen-and-ink
with digitally applied color.
www.holidayhouse.com
First Edition
1 3 5 7 9 10 8 6 4 2

Library of Congress Cataloging-in-Publication Data
Janovitz, Marilyn.
I will try / Marilyn Janovitz. — 1st ed.
p. cm. — (I like to read)
Summary: A young girl beginning to learn gymnastics is tempted to quit
because she cannot spin and jump like her friend Jan, but Jan
persuades her to keep trying.
ISBN 978-0-8234-2399-6 (hardcover)
[1. Determination (Personality trait)—Fiction. 2. Gymnastics—Fiction.
3. Friendship—Fiction.] I. Title.
PZ7.J2446Iam 2012
[E]—dc22
2011005020

I eat.

Then I brush.

I pack my bag.

"Time to go," says Dad.

"Have fun," says Mom.

Oh! It is Jan.

I like her.

Jan can do a split.

Jan can pose.

Jan can jump.

Jan can spin.

Can I?

I will try.

"Oh, no!"

Down I go.

I give up.

"Don't give up," says Jan.

"Try again."

I try again.

I did it!

"Thank you, Jan!"

I Like to Read™ Books
You will like all of them!

Boy, Bird, and Dog *by David McPhail*

Dinosaurs Don't, Dinosaurs Do
by Steve Björkman

Fish Had a Wish *by Michael Garland*

I Will Try *by Marilyn Janovitz*

The Lion and the Mice
by Rebecca Emberley and Ed Emberley

See Me Run *by Paul Meisel*